Kisses for Later

story by
Jenn Zahavich

illustrations by
Julie-Lynn Zahavich

Coady was a special boy.

Coady had big blue eyes and shiny blond hair. He loved to give hugs that squeezed and he had tiny dimples on his cheeks that magically appeared when he laughed.

Coady was so excited when he turned three years old, because he loved to say, "Hey, I'm free." He would hold up all of those fingers, and proudly tell anyone who asked, "I'm free!"

Some days, Coady was a robot. He would walk stiffly around the house and repeat in a robot voice, "Rrrrr, rrrrr, I am a robot. Rrrrr, rrrrr, rrrrr."

Some days, Coady was a pirate. He would pull a black plastic patch over his eye and tramp around the house growling, "Arrgh, Matey. Walk the plank! In with the sharks! Arrgh!"

Some days, Coady was simply Super Coady. He would tie his red cape around his neck and spend afternoons jumping from the couch to the chair in the living room. Actually, *most* days were Super Coady days.

The best part about being a robot or a pirate or Super Coady was that Coady's mom always remembered to charge his battery, or shine his patch, or mend any tears in his cape. Coady and his mom were best friends. They did everything together. She always held up the rocks while Coady looked for crabs at the beach. She made the best rocketships out of boxes—they even had fire at the bottom. And she always made him feel better if he got a bump or a scratch. Mom's kisses were simply the best medicine.

One day, Coady was so excited. He was going to school like a big boy, all by himself!

In the morning he kissed his mom goodbye and ran out the door. He climbed into Dad's truck as fast as he could. He could hardly wait to get to school.

When they arrived, Dad gave Coady a big hug. He was so proud of his special boy.

Coady hung up his cape on his very own hook. When he looked around, he noticed that some kids were colouring and some were blowing bubbles. Some of them were jumping in the jumping room. A few of them were dressed up like doctors, and one was even dressed up like a dinosaur. Coady could hardly believe his eyes. This was going to be the best day ever!

"Hi, Coady," said his teacher. "My name is Cheril. How old are you?"

Coady proudly pulled out those three favourite fingers and with a big smile he said, "I'm free."

"Fantastic!" said Cheril. "I love people who are free. Come on in."

Dad waved goodbye. "See you later, Buddy."

"Bye Dad!" said Coady. He already had one leg in a lion costume. "I'm a lion! Rrrroar!"

That afternoon, Mom was getting excited to see Coady. She had missed him all day and she was looking forward to hearing about the fun he had at school. When Dad's truck pulled into the driveway, she watched as Coady climbed out of his seat and slowly made his way toward the front door.

Mom couldn't wait—she swung open the front door. "Hi, Super Coady!" she exclaimed. "I missed you. How was your first day of school?"

Coady looked sad.

"Are you okay?" asked Mom.

"Mom," said Coady in a small, shaky voice. "Today at school I got a hurt and I missed you. I was sad."

"Oh," said Mom. "Come here Little Guy, I know just what you need. Give me your hand. Put your finger up here behind your ear. Do you feel that little space back there, the little spot between your ear and your neck? A space just big enough for your finger to fit in?"

"Yeah," said Coady.

"I'll tell you what," said Mom. "I'm going to fill that spot up with kisses, and we will keep it full. That way, if you ever fall or get hurt and I'm not around, all you have to do is put your finger up there and grab a kiss. Put that kiss wherever your hurt is, and you will feel better. I promise. Should we practice?"

"Yes," said Coady.

Mom leaned over and poked Coady in the leg.

"Ouch!" said Coady.

"Did that hurt a bit?" asked Mom.

"A bit," said the little free-year-old.

"Okay, what should you do?" asked Mom.

Coady looked into his mom's eyes and smiled a little smile. He slowly lifted his hand up to his ear. Mom watched him, and his eyes grew wide.

"I got one," he whispered. His hand came down with a kiss pinched between his thumb and his finger and he carefully placed it on his poked leg. He let out a little gasp. "Mom, it worked! I feel better!"

"See, I told you," said Mom. "We just have to remember to keep the kisses full."

"Mom, can you read me a story?" asked Coady.

"Of course I can," Mom replied. "I love you, Coady."

"I love you too, Mom."

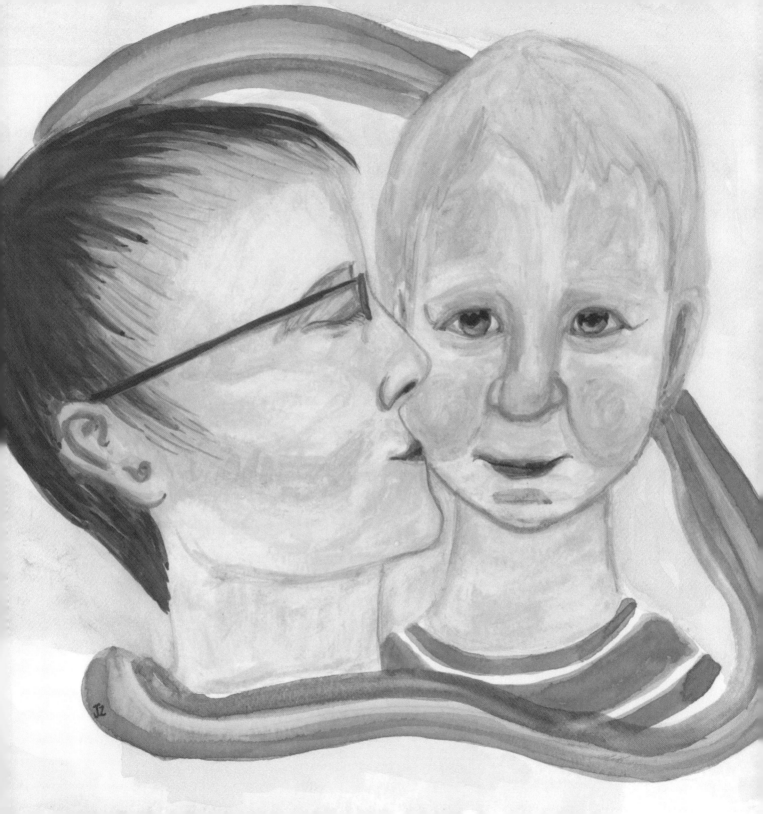

That night, Mom stood outside Coady's bedroom door and listened while Dad tucked him into bed. Coady told Dad all about the special hiding spot he had for Mom's kisses.

"That's fantastic!" said Dad. "Can I put some behind your other ear?"

"Sure!" said Coady.

Mom listened as Dad leaned over and filled up the other side.

The next morning, after a good night's sleep, Mom heard Coady's toes hit the floor. As the door to Mom and Dad's room creaked open slowly, that special little blue-eyed, shiny-haired Super Coady softly stepped into the room.

"Good morning," he whispered.

"Good morning," said Mom and Dad.

"Are you ready for another fun day at school today?" asked Dad.

"Yes, I am!" said Coady excitedly. "I'm going to be a doctor today."

"Wow," said Mom. "That sounds like fun."

"Yep," said Coady. "Mom? Could you fill up my kisses before I go?"

"You bet, Sweetheart," said Mom. "Come on over here. My favourite job in the whole world is to fill up your kisses."

Mom leaned in close and gently nuzzled into that tiny space behind the little free-year-old ear. She softly kissed about a hundred kisses. When she was finished she took a deep breath and breathed in the sweetness of her special free-year-old with the big blue eyes and the magic dimples.

Now they were both ready for a new beautiful day and any of the bumps that came with it.

"Have a good day, Super Coady," said Mom.

"Mom, I'm not Super Coady. I'm a doctor!" said Coady in a very serious voice.

"Oh," said Mom. "I'm sorry. Well, Dr. Coady, remember that you are a special boy, and you are so loved."

Dr. Coady stepped out the front door. Shortly after, Mom watched as the door reopened and a little free-year-old came back inside and around the corner.

Coady looked up and said, "Thanks for the kisses, Mom. Could you hand me my cape?"

FriesenPress

Suite 300 - 990 Fort St
Victoria, BC, Canada, V8V 3K2
www.friesenpress.com

Library and Archives Canada Cataloguing in Publication

Zahavich, Jenn, 1979-, author
Kisses for later / story by Jenn Zahavich;
illustrated by Julie-Lynn Zahavich.

Issued in print and electronic formats.
ISBN 978-1-4602-5991-7 (pbk.).—ISBN 978-1-4602-5992-4 (pdf)

I. Zahavich, Julie-Lynn, 1988-, illustrator II. Title.

PS8649.A925K58 2015   jC813'.6   C2015-901633-9
                                        C2015-901634-7

1. Juvenile Fiction, Family

Distributed to the trade by The Ingram Book Company

Jenn Zahavich had a way with words. For the duration of her two-year battle with cancer she opened up her heart to family, friends, and strangers. She did this through an online blog that connected a community. She shared her story, the ups and the downs, and taught everyone around her how to spread love each and every day.

Much of Jenn's inspiration was a result of her beautiful son Coady. She often said she could see her reflection in the deep blue of his eyes. She never realized just how deeply she could love before Coady. It's not much wonder sweet Coady was Jenn's inspiration for writing *Kisses for Later* in the midst of her cancer treatment.

One afternoon when Jenn was driving home from a doctor's appointment, a story came through the sky and literally went right through her. She drove directly to her friend's house and asked for a piece of paper and a pen. She sat down at the kitchen table and wrote her story, word for word. She knew she had created something extraordinary.

Jenn passed away in March 2011, before this book could be illustrated by her sister Julie-Lynn, and launched into the market; however, her family has taken great pride in working hard over the past few years to turn Jenn's dream into a reality. This book is for Coady and for everyone coast to coast, from one Island to the other, who knew and loved Jenn.

To learn more about Jenn's story, visit:
www.babywillyoulovemewhenimbald.blogspot.ca

CPSIA information can be obtained at www.ICGtesting.com
Printed in the USA
LVIW01n1911040815
448802LV00007B/117

* 9 7 8 1 4 6 0 2 5 9 9 1 7 *